Goldilocks and the ~~Three Puppies~~

Goldilocks and the ~~Three Naked Mole Rats~~

~~Go~~ T...

...cks and the ~~Cavemen~~

Goldilocks and the ~~Three Whales~~

~~Goldilocks and the Three Giraffes~~

Gold... T...

~~Goldilocks and the Three Mosquitoes~~

~~Goldilocks and the Three Lions~~

~~Goldilocks and the Three Moles~~

...the ...s

~~Goldilocks and the Three Terrible Monsters~~

~~Goldilocks and the Three Apes~~

Goldilocks a... Three Prir...

~~...cks and the ...e Geese~~

~~Goldilocks and the Three Giants~~

~~Goldilocks and the Three Chickens~~

~~Gol... T...~~

...the ...es

~~Goldilocks and the Three Penguins~~

~~Goldilocks and the Three Cyclopes~~

Goldilocks a... Three M...

~~...cks and the ...e Bunnies~~

~~Goldilocks and the Three Dogs~~

~~Goldilocks and the Three Germans~~

Gol... T...

...he

~~Goldilocks and the Three Goldfish~~

~~Goldilocks and the Three Pumas~~

~~Goldilocks a... Three Tig...~~

~~...ks and the ...e Nutrias~~

~~Goldilocks and the Three Rocket Scientists~~

~~Goldilocks and the Three Ants~~

Gold... T...

...he

~~Goldilocks and the Three Meerkats~~

~~Goldilocks and the Three Goats~~

~~Goldilocks a... Three Co...~~

~~...ks and the ...Big Feet~~

~~Gold... Th...~~

~~Goldilocks and the Three Wild Boars~~

~~Gol... T...~~

GOLDILOCKS

and the

THREE
DINOSAURS

As Retold by

MO WILLEMS

WALKER BOOKS
AND SUBSIDIARIES
LONDON · BOSTON · SYDNEY · AUCKLAND

ONCE UPON A TIME, there were three Dinosaurs:
Papa Dinosaur, Mama Dinosaur and some other Dinosaur
who happened to be visiting from Norway.

One day, for no particular reason, the three Dinosaurs
made up their beds, positioned their chairs just so
and cooked three bowls of delicious chocolate
pudding at varying temperatures.

"OH BOY!" said Papa Dinosaur in his loud, booming voice.
"IT IS FINALLY TIME TO LEAVE AND GO TO
THE … uhhh … SOME PLACE ELSE!"

"YES!" continued Mama Dinosaur. "I HOPE NO INNOCENT LITTLE SUCCULENT CHILD HAPPENS BY OUR UNLOCKED HOME WHILE WE ARE … uhhh … SOME PLACE ELSE!"

Then the other Dinosaur made a loud noise that sounded like a big, evil laugh but was probably just a polite Norwegian expression.

The three Dinosaurs went Someplace Else and were definitely *not* hiding in the woods waiting for an unsuspecting child to come by.

Sure enough, five minutes later a poorly supervised little girl named Goldilocks came traipsing along.

Just then the forest boomed with what could
have been a Dinosaur yelling "GOTCHA!", but
I'm pretty sure was just the wind.

The loud noise was immediately followed by
another loud noise that sounded kind of like,
"BE PATIENT, PAPA DINOSAUR!
THE TRAP IS NOT YET SPRUNG!"

But that could have been a
rock falling. Or a squirrel.

GETTING
CLOSER!

Either way, Goldilocks was not the type of little
girl who listened to anyone or anything.

For example, Goldilocks never listened to warnings about
the dangers of barging into strange, enormous houses.

So as soon as Goldilocks came
across a strange, enormous house,
she barged right in.

WELCOME
(Tee-Hee!)

Inside, Goldilocks immediately smelled the three bowls of delicious chocolate pudding.

"Mmmmm!" said Goldilocks. "That chocolate pudding smells delicious. If only I could get all the way up to the top of that counter!"

Then Goldilocks noticed a very tall ladder that just happened to be there and certainly wasn't left on purpose.

Goldilocks climbed up the ladder
and found herself face-to-face
with three gigantic bowls
of chocolate pudding.

The first bowl of chocolate pudding was too hot,
but Goldilocks ate it all anyway because,
hey, it's chocolate pudding, right?

The second bowl of chocolate pudding was too cold,
but who cares about temperature when you've got
a big bowl of chocolate pudding?

Not her.

The third bowl of chocolate pudding was *just right*, but Goldilocks was on such a roll by now, she hardly noticed.

Soon Goldilocks was stuffed like one of
those delicious chocolate-filled-little-girl-bonbons
(which, by the way, are totally *not* the favourite
things in the whole world for hungry Dinosaurs).

Tired and groggy, Goldilocks noticed three chairs
in the living room. So she climbed down the
ladder and walked out of the kitchen.

The first chair was too tall.

The second chair was too tall.

But the *third* chair —

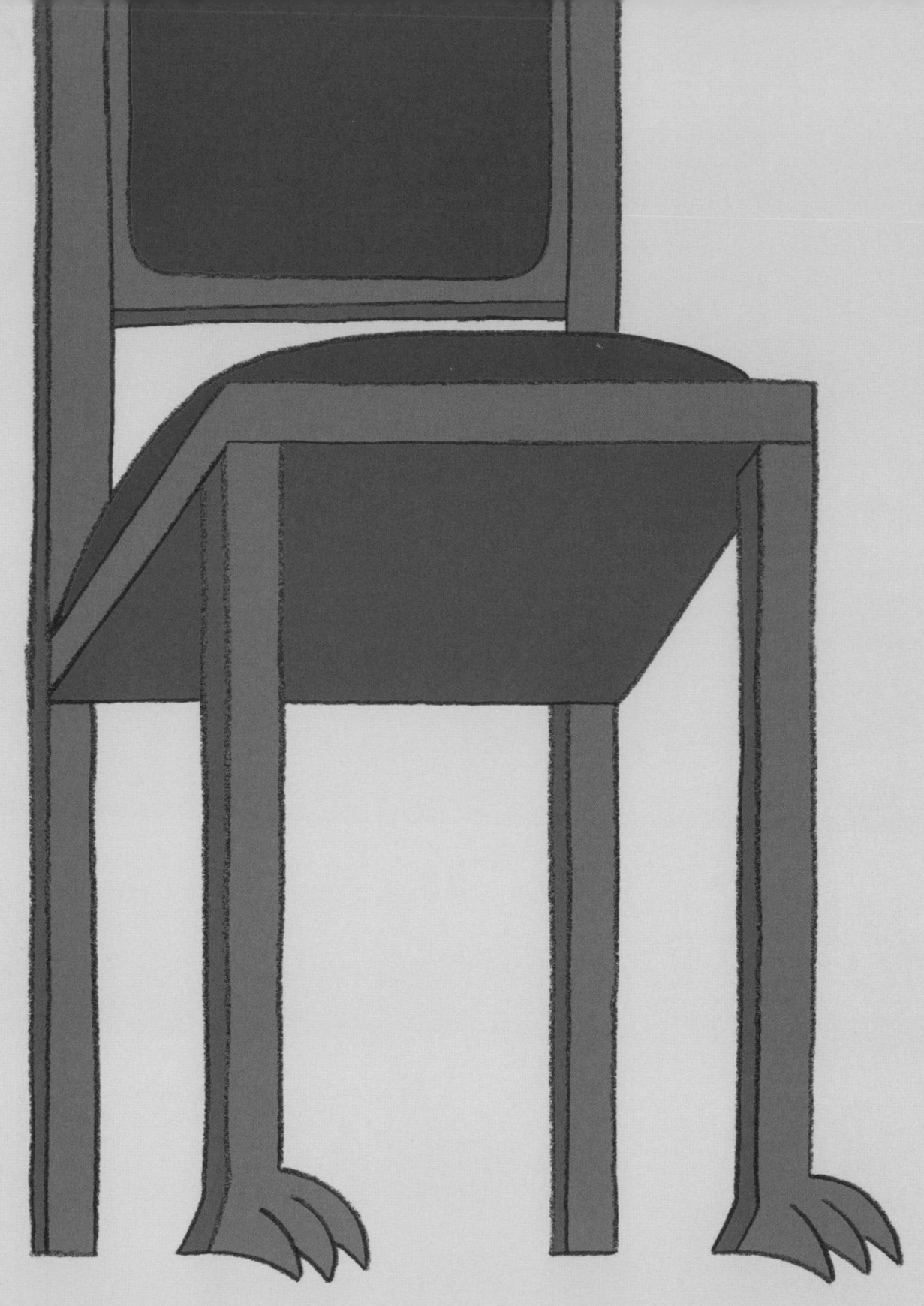

WAS TOO TALL.
Goldilocks wasn't going to climb that high just to sit
in some chair, so she trekked over to the bedroom.

When she got there, Goldilocks noticed that the beds were also gigantically big. "What is going on around here!?" groaned the exhausted girl. "The bears that live here must be nuts!"

Just then the room filled with a loud, booming noise that
was either a passing truck or a Dinosaur gloating,

"A FEW MORE MINUTES AND
SHE'LL BE ASLEEP! DELICIOUS
CHOCOLATE-FILLED-LITTLE-GIRL-
BONBONS ARE YUMMIER WHEN
THEY'RE RESTED!"

Even a little girl who never listens to
anyone or anything had to hear *that*.

HOME SWEET DiNOSAU→ HOME

Goldilocks took a minute to stop and think, which was longer than she was used to stopping and thinking.

"Hey…" she told herself. "This isn't some bear's house. This is some DINOSAUR'S house!"

Say what you like about Goldilocks,
but she was no fool. As quickly as she could,
she ran to the back door and *got out of there!*

Just then a loud plane flew by, which sounded pretty much like a trio of Dinosaurs yelling "NOW!" or "CHARGE!" or the Norwegian expression for "CHEWY-BONBON-TIME!"

Suddenly – and completely coincidentally – the three Dinosaurs rushed through the front door.

But they were too late.

Goldilocks was gone, and all that was left in the house were three disappointed Dinosaurs.

And the moral is:

If you ever find yourself
in the wrong story, leave.

And the moral for Dinosaurs is:

LOCK THE BACK DOOR!

Goldilocks and the Three Musketeers

Goldilocks and the Three Free Men

Goldilocks and the Three Xylophones

...cks and the ...ee Poodles

Goldilocks and the Three Dudes

Goldilocks and the Three Red Herring

Go...

Goldilocks and the Three Wall Street Types

Goldilocks and the Three Crows

Goldilocks and the Three Owls

...the

Goldilocks and the Three Bus Drivers

Goldilocks and the Three Termites

Goldilocks Three H...

...cks and the ...ee Worms

Goldilocks and the Three Drummers

Goldilocks and the Three Wise Men

Go... T...

...the ...es

Goldilocks and the Three Condors

Goldilocks and the Three Rats

Goldilocks Three Major...

Dedicated to Lee and Diane, dinosaurs

First published in Great Britain 2013 by Walker Books Ltd, 87 Vauxhall Walk, London SE11 5HJ

10 9 8 7 6 5 4 3 2 1   ❖   Copyright © 2013 Mo Willems

First published in the United States 2012 by Balzer + Bray, an imprint of HarperCollins Publishers.
British publication rights arranged with Wernick & Pratt Agency, LLC.
The right of Mo Willems to be identified as author/illustrator of this work has been
asserted by him in accordance with the Copyright, Designs and Patents Act 1988.

This book has been typeset in Windsor Light   ❖   Printed in China

British Library Cataloguing in Publication Data:
a catalogue record for this book is available from the British Library.

ISBN 978-1-4063-4729-6   ❖   www.walker.co.uk   ❖   Visit www.mowillems.com

...locks and the ...ee Squid

Goldilocks T...

...the

Goldilocks Three Glasse...

...ocks and the ...ee Gerbils

Go...

...the ...ls

Goldilocks and the Three Foot-Long Hoagies

Goldilocks and the Three Prairie Dogs

Goldilocks Three-Pied...

...ocks and the ...ee Bedbugs

Goldilocks and the Three Frogs

Goldilocks and the Three Deer

Go...